Little Bear's Big Adventure

written by Kathleen Allan Meyer

illustrated by Carole Boerke

Library of Congress Catalog Card Number 89-52033
Copyright © 1990 by Kathleen Allan Meyer
Published by The STANDARD PUBLISHING Company, Cincinnati, Ohio
Division of STANDEX INTERNATIONAL Corporation. Printed in U.S.A.

Little Bear sat on the tree stump
beside his front door. It was a lovely
spring day in the forest, but Little Bear
wasn't very happy.

"What's there to do around here?" he
asked himself. And he was so tired of
hearing his mother say, "Please stay
right outside the front door, Little Bear.
Don't go away."

Then his brothers, Beartram and Alfred, would always chime in, "And you're too little to come with us!"

"I need a big adventure," Little Bear
said to himself. "Then maybe I'll feel big
and brave!"

Just then two of his friends came
along the path.

"Come with us today, Little Bear,"
they called to him. "The first thing
we're going to do is go fishing in Big
River."

"Great!" said Little Bear, "I've never
been to Big River. My mother has only
taken me to Little Pond."

Then he turned and looked in the kitchen window. His mother was busy. She wasn't watching him.

Good, he thought, *now I can start out on my big adventure! Mother will never know.*

Little Bear's eyes opened wide when
they came to Big River. The water was
tumbling along swiftly. He watched it
splashing over huge boulders.

Little Bear and his friends fished for
a little while from the shore, but they
didn't have any luck.

"Why don't you wade out into the
middle of the river, Little Bear," one of
his friends suggested. "Maybe you could
catch a nice big fish there for us to
share."

"I'll try," replied Little Bear happily.

He was very pleased that his friends
had asked him to do this. It *was* a big
adventure! His mother would never have
allowed it.

Bravely Little Bear waded into the
river. Then he felt the strong current
tug at his legs. Kerplunk! Head over
heels he went, down under the icy
water. And Little Bear wasn't the
world's greatest swimmer yet!

Suddenly he hit a large log sticking out from shore. Little Bear grabbed it and pulled himself up.

"Better luck next time!" said his friends as they stood there laughing at him. Then they started down the path once again.

Feeling rather cold and wet, Little
Bear followed along behind them. Soon
they came to a big patch of blueberries.
They all began to eat.

"I'd like to take some of these home
for my mother's blueberry cookies,"
Little Bear said.

"Never mind about that, Little Bear,"
they told him, "just keep eating."

So he ate and ate and ate until he began
to feel quite sick.

"Get up, Little Bear," his friends said,
"we have another fun thing to do."

By this time Little Bear wondered if all
of this *was* so much fun!

But he got up and followed them.
Soon they led him to a big field dotted
with little boxes.

"What are those?" asked Little Bear.
He had never before been this far away
from home to see such things.

"Those are the farmer's beehives.
They're filled with delicious honey!" his
friends answered.

Now Little Bear had only seen the
honeycombs his mother brought home
from the forest. He especially
remembered the big one at the
Valentine party.

"Why don't you walk over there and bring back one of those boxes?" suggested his two friends. "Then we can all share some honey."

So Little Bear started to walk into
the field. Then, as fast as you can say
"Jack Robinson," he turned to his
friends.

"No!" he called out to them. "I've been
in enough trouble today! I don't need to
do what you tell me to."

Then he headed back down the path
toward home. He felt braver at that
moment than he had all day!

But at the same time, Little Bear was
sorry that he had disobeyed his mother.
And he would tell her that when he
reached home.

For in his heart Little Bear knew she
was right. Little adventures were *still*
best for him after all!